Buzz Buzz, Bumble Kitty

Nick Sharratt

BARRON'S

Buzz buzz, bumble bee

Howdy!

A wild West

Meow!
A striped

Wow!

A skyscraper

Spikey!

A juicy

Oh dear! A royal

Yippee!

A wibbly, wobbly

Whirrrr!
A heli-

Rattle!

An adorable

Eggcellent!
A boiled

Whoosh!
A spouting

cowboy

kitty

building

pineapple

queen

dessert

copter

baby

egg

whale

First edition for the United States and Canada published 2000
by Barron's Educational Series, Inc.

First published in the UK by Scholastic Ltd. 2000

All inquiries should be addressed to:
Barron's Educational Series, Inc.
250 Wireless Boulevard
Hauppauge, NY 11788
http://www.barronseduc.com

International Standard Book No.: 0-7641-5233-5

Library of Congress Catalog Card No.: 99-66184

Printed and bound in China

9 8 7 6 5 4 3 2 1